Part 1 JF LEV
LeVasseur, Brent.
Aoleon the Martian girl. Part one, First
contact / Brent LeVasseur.

The Martian Girl

PART ONE

**This is Part One of a five-part series.
Parts One through five are:**

*Aoléon The Martian Girl – Part 1: First Contact*

*Aoléon The Martian Girl – Part 2: The Luminess of Mars*

*Aoléon The Martian Girl – Part 3: The Hollow Moon*

*Aoléon The Martian Girl – Part 4: Illegal Aliens*

*Aoléon The Martian Girl – Part 5: The Great Pyramid of Cydonia*

# AOLÉON

## The Martian Girl

### PART ONE

# Brent LeVasseur

*For all media inquiries, publishing, merchandising, or licensing:*
*aoleon@aoleonthemartiangirl.com*

For information regarding permissions, e-mail Aoléon USA at:
aoleon@aoleonthemartiangirl.com
or use the Contact Us page at:
http://aoleonthemartiangirl.com

Visit Aoléon The Martian Girl website for more information at:
http://aoleonthemartiangirl.com.

ISBN Hardcover: 978-0-9791285-2-3
ISBN Paperback: 978-0-9791285-1-6
ISBN eBook: 978-0-9791285-0-9

Published in the U.S.A.

**Welcome to Part 1 of a five-part series.**

# TABLE OF CONTENTS

# DREAMS
## CHAPTER ONE

## SULLIVAN FARM HOUSE
## NEBRASKA, UNITED STATES
## PLANET EARTH

Gilbert Sullivan often had strange dreams the night before the circle makers came. And this night was no different. Fear shot through Gilbert's veins. They were coming.

"Hurry up and get this portal open!" cried a familiar female voice.

"We've got company!" shouted Gilbert.

"Stand to and return fire!" ordered a male voice.

Robotic spider-like legs scraped the floor. Gilbert turned in time to see two pulse-cannons attached to pincers track toward him. Flashes and a deep *thrum* shook and blinded him as bursts of molten plasma struck his chest.

Then nothing.

Gilbert opened his eyes and bolted upright in bed. Another nightmare. The third one this week. And — incredibly — the same every time.

*Ha! I'm still alive,* thought Gilbert. He wiped the sweat off his brow with his pajama sleeve. He was still keyed up — on high alert as if something lurking in the shadows might jump out at him at any moment. He scanned the room for danger signs.

Brilliant beams of moonlight glistened in through his far bedroom window. A tree swayed in the breeze outside, forming shadows that danced across his bedspread. The full moon in plain view cast its rays onto various toy action figures, miniature vehicles and wooden building blocks that lay strewn about his bedroom floor. An eleven-inch telescope stood by the open window in the far corner painted by moonbeams. Xena, a kitty cat and Gilbert's good friend, had leapt onto the top of his dresser.

Gradually Gilbert accepted that he was back in his own bedroom and safe in bed. Sucking in a deep breath, Gilbert slowly became calmer and lay down. His thoughts drifted.

A mysterious crop-circle formation had appeared on his neighbor's farm just last summer and sparked Gilbert's interest in space and astronomy. It also marked the beginning of these dreams. He considered whether it just might be a coincidence that these strange crop circles kept appearing in his neighbor's field on the same nights he had these dreams. All the local newspapers reported seeing strange lights in the night sky before the crop circles appeared. But that wasn't enough to give him nightmares — especially ones about giant killer robots chasing him.

These nightmares were starting to gnaw away at him. He hadn't had a good night's sleep in weeks, and his work on the farm had begun to suffer. Something was triggering these dreams, but he was unsure of what it could be. His mother had accused him of playing too many video games over at his best friend Dugan's house. But that wasn't completely true because he had spent most of his time playing outside.

Old Farmer Neville Johnson, Gilbert's neighbor and owner of the field that had been "vandalized" by "so-called aliens," told news reporters that the crop circles were most likely created by pranksters playing tricks. Gilbert happened to be at the top of his list of suspects. Not to mention that the local news had dismissed the reports, and the U.S. Air Force had made a statement claiming they were testing some new type of weather balloon and had been dropping illumination flares. That was their rationale for people claiming to see strange lights in the sky. But it didn't explain how the crop circles had appeared, and to anyone who had witnessed the lights, it seemed like a feeble attempt to explain away something incredible.

Gilbert was now completely awake, so he decided to get up. He listened to the sounds of a typical Nebraskan summer night drifting through his open window — crickets chirping and leaves rustling, occasionally accented by the uneven taps of his window shutters, which were blown by puffs of wind and were slapping against the side of the farmhouse. The peaceful sounds were disturbed by muffled yells and the occasional slamming of a door downstairs.

*They're fighting…again,* he thought as he exhaled through his teeth. His fears about his parents possibly getting a divorce entered his thoughts. Now sleepless, Gilbert walked over to his telescope and peered through its lens. Moonlight illuminated his backyard making the softly swaying shadows from the trees come alive.

Gilbert carefully rotated the focus knob on his telescope, tracking a distant star in the Pleiades cluster that was a part

of the Taurus Constellation. In the background, he could still hear his parents arguing downstairs. Xena swished her tail and rubbed against Gilbert's legs, craving attention. He stroked her soft grey-and-white-striped fur while whispering to her. "I wish I could be in a place where there isn't any trouble. Take me some place far, far away — beyond the Moon, or past that star."

Xena mewed, looking up at him as if she had understood him, affectionately rubbing her fuzzy face against his hand. As Gilbert gazed through his telescope, he closed his eyes and made a prayerful wish. "Please send me an angel to take me away from here."

As he said the words, an image flashed into Gilbert's mind — streaks of stars and galaxies moving in a blur and a small ship quickly flying through them. In that moment, he somehow knew that his prayer had been answered. The ship was coming for him.

# FIRST CONTACT
## CHAPTER TWO

# UNIVERSAL CENTER
# (OR THEREABOUTS)

The saucer sped through deep space. It was a small ship about the size of a sports car, and its semitransparent metallic hull was colored baby blue. An incredibly powerful plasma-induced gravimetric force field surrounded the ship, so intense that it flared pulses of circular, glowing

rainbows, creating a parhelion effect around the craft. The ship shot right and left, up and down, back and forth — the way a humming bird darts from one flower to the next. Except in this case, flowers were galaxies, and the distances traveled in an instant were beyond calculation. After passing through the core of several galaxies, the ship approached a spiral galaxy: The Milky Way. Home.

The ship began to slow as it pierced several large nebulae — gaseous clouds that scintillated and mushroomed past the ship in bursts of red, yellow, orange and blue. The saucer flew through the Pillars of Creation in the Eagle Nebula and past several stars that bloomed bright in passing before it entered our solar system. It flew past Saturn, slicing directly through its dust and ice-ridden rings that sparkled with light, past Jupiter with its great red spot of a slowly spinning vortex of multicolored gases, past the asteroid belt, and past Mars. It paused for a brief moment above the Earth to take in the view of the sun setting over the Earth's ecliptic, which exploded creating a large elliptical bloom that became bloated and distorted by the Earth's atmosphere and finally dissolved into darkness. The ship dropped rapidly, descending to the surface of the planet.

*"Woooeee!"* the alien visitor exclaimed, giggling to herself with excitement. The saucer swooped down through the clouds, began a low-level flight over the Midwest United States, and headed toward Nebraska. It was dusk, and a full harvest moon shone as the sun set in the west creating an explosion of orange and red, a sharp contrast to a darkening azure sky. The stars seemed to twinkle a little brighter as if performing a dance, and the lights from the cities below resembled a sea filled with glowing phosphorescence.

The visitor flew her saucer in low-level passes over a wheat field, looking for the perfect spot to begin her real fun — making crop circles. She could cause the wheat to bend into any pattern she wanted just by imagining it. The

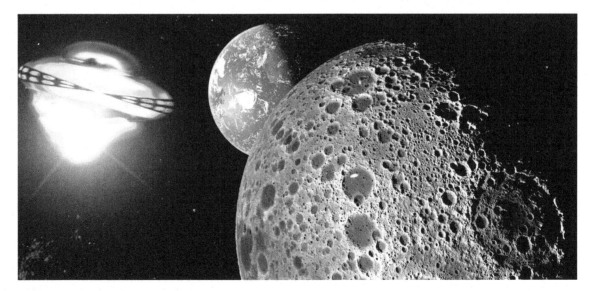

ship and all of its controls were linked to her by thought alone. After the electromagnetic beam activated, she could think of any shape she wanted, and the beam would ionize the wheat into a crop-circle pattern the way a magnet pulls metal shavings. The ionization would bend the wheat at the root, leaving the wheat undamaged. As a result, it would continue to grow in its bent-over position long after she was gone — something that any crop-circle expert would tell you is impossible for humans to fake.

First, she decided to create overlapping circles forming a pyramid shape in the middle. The pyramid just happened to be the emblem of the Martian Space Academy. Next, she made an intricate spiraling Mandelbrot set with repeating patterns getting smaller and smaller as they spiraled inward toward the center. She employed various forms of sacred geometry arranged in complex patterns to create her imagery — merging the languages of art with mathematics to convey her subtle message to the peoples of Terra — I am here…I am intelligent…and *I am not of this Earth!* Only a herd of cows took notice of her strange nocturnal activities. They watched her curiously while grazing in a nearby pasture.

ⓞ ⓞ ⓞ

# MCCONNELL AIR FORCE BASE WICHITA, KANSAS, UNITED STATES PLANET EARTH

Stationed at McConnell Air Force Base in Kansas, Airman Buzz, an eighteen-year-old radar controller, sat in an Air Force Early Warning System control room playing a video game instead of watching his radar screen when a blip appeared on the scope. His job was to observe and track domestic air traffic over the midwestern United States. The radar had started to beep, indicating that there was a contact — something of interest to be checked out. But by the time he took his eyes off the game, the contact had disappeared. "Dang glitches," grumbled the controller. He tapped the radar screen twice as if that would somehow magically make the contact reappear. When nothing happened, he went back to playing his game, a bit annoyed that his character had died and he had to start the level over again.

# ◉◉◉

## SULLIVAN FARM HOUSE
## NEBRASKA, UNITED STATES
## PLANET EARTH

**B**ack in Nebraska, Gilbert was looking through his telescope at another constellation when a star that was not visible a moment ago began to move slowly and increase in brightness. "Wait a second…" Gilbert watched as it grew brighter and brighter. "That's no star!" Gilbert became alert — his subconscious prodded him to pay attention to a small but important detail that his conscious mind was too overwhelmed to notice. It wasn't a sound that made him uneasy; it was the sudden *lack* of sound that sent a prickly sensation running up and down his spine.

The trees were still moving — without making any noise. Everything had become very, very quiet. The shutters stopped slapping, the trees stopped swishing, and the crickets stopped chirping. It was as if he had suddenly stepped into a vacuum where no noise was possible except for the sound of his thumping heart. The star quickly increased in size and shot over Gilbert's farmhouse. The light from the object became so bright that it temporarily blinded him. For a split second, Gilbert's entire bedroom lit up as if the roof had been torn off his house and the midday sun shone down upon him. The object passed directly overhead. Yet there was absolutely no sound at all. It was still the middle of the night, and darkness returned to his bedroom. "Oh my gosh!" Gilbert gasped, half falling out of his chair.

The blood drained from Gilbert's face. His body tensed. Feeling woozy, he stood up, turned around too quickly, tripped over some toys, and fell flat on his face with a loud thud. He picked himself up, composed himself, and looked around with embarrassment. Xena, bemused, watched him from her perch atop his dresser.

After tearing off his slippers, bathrobe and pajamas, Gilbert quickly donned his farm-boy overalls, blue sweat-shirt, jacket, cowboy hat, and boots. Grabbing his flashlight and snatching a candy bar from the top of his dresser, he gave Xena a quick kiss on her head. On his way out the door, he stopped briefly to peer at himself in the mirror. He inhaled deeply, mustering his courage, checked his gear one last time, and saluted to himself in the mirror. Stealthily he crept downstairs, taking extra care to avoid the creaky step near the bottom of the staircase. He tiptoed past the kitchen door where his parents were still arguing, opened the back door to the house, and exited, closing the door carefully and quietly behind him.

The moon lit his backyard with a soft glow that made the shadows of the surrounding trees and farmhouse seem alive. He gazed at the stars in the night sky, searching for anything out of the ordinary, and then scanned his backyard before proceeding. He crept silently over a small hill and climbed carefully over the old wooden fence that separated his backyard from the adjoining wheat fields. He saw a strange, glowing light in the far distance. "What could that possibly be?" He rubbed his eyes to make sure he wasn't dreaming. Realizing that this wasn't a dream, he fought his instincts to turn back. Curiosity ultimately overcame his fear; he decided to soldier on.

ⓞⓞⓞ

## JOHNSON WHEAT FIELD
## NEBRASKA, UNITED STATES
## PLANET EARTH

He crept into the wheat field and headed toward the light. The field was doused in warm, moonlit air. From the wheat came the sound of boots scuffling through the underbrush. The wheat rose up to his nose, partially obstructing his view. He could now see the strange glow from multicolored pulsating lights that illuminated the sky. It was as if he were viewing the light show from an outdoor rock concert, except no sound accompanied the light's rhythmic beating. He kept moving quietly. The only sound he could hear was his own breath punctuated by the crunching of his footsteps through the thick strands of wheat and moist earth.

Minutes passed as he advanced through the field, but to him it seemed like hours. Gilbert clung to the shadows and kept advancing. In the distance, the strange light pulsed, changing hue with each beat like fingers reaching skyward, growing steadily brighter. His heart leapt in anticipation of what he might find when he arrived at the source.

The light now glowed brilliantly. He knew he was getting close to its source because he could feel a deep thrumming that vibrated the ground underneath his feet. He slowed his pace to advance more quietly for fear of being discovered. He watched the colors shift in hue from red to blue to yellow to purple and back again, each time growing a bit brighter.

# ⊙⊙⊙

## JOHNSON FARMHOUSE
## NEBRASKA, UNITED STATES
## PLANET EARTH

Gilbert wasn't the only one who had noticed the light. Mrs. Johnson, Farmer Johnson's wife, was a light sleeper and awoke when the bright light flooded her bedroom. At first, she thought that she might have overslept and that it was the morning sun. Glancing at her clock, she discovered it was still the middle of the night and instantly became worried. Sitting up, she tried to nudge her husband awake, but he didn't stir. She nudged him again to no avail.

"Did you hear something? Listen!" The only sound was her husband's snores. Mrs. Johnson shook him again, a little harder this time. "Do you see that light outside? Wake up!" Farmer Johnson mumbled something in his sleep and began to snore again. She shook him even harder.

"Huh? Oh, it's nothing. Go back to sleep," mumbled Farmer Johnson.

Just then Mrs. Johnson heard a strange noise outside, the lights pulsating brighter than before. "Wake up! Did you hear that? Look…lights!"

"I'll check in the morning, dear." Farmer Johnson responded groggily, turning on his side and pulling the covers up over his head. He began to snore again.

"Wake up! There's something strange going on outside in our field!" Finally, Mrs. Johnson crawled out of bed, fetched a bucket of water, and threw it on her slumbering husband. Farmer Johnson leapt out of bed, tripped over his slippers and crashed face-first into the bedroom door. As he got back up, drenched, the bookshelves on the wall behind him collapsed, covering him in a pile of books. Slowly he dug himself out from under the pile and stood up, wondering what was going on.

"Woman, what in God's name has gotten into you?"

"Look! Look! See the lights there? Someone is in our field! It could be vandals or looters."

"All right," he said, shrugging his shoulders, annoyed.

He pulled on his work boots, grabbed his shotgun and called his hound dog, Tripod, who came hobbling over to him. Tripod (whose name used to be Oscar before the accident) was a basset hound with a large black nose, sausage-shaped body, and three short squat legs. (He lost one of his legs in a hunting accident when Farmer Johnson fired at a pheasant and shot him instead.)

Farmer Johnson threw his coat on over his nightshirt and headed out, slamming the rickety screen door behind him such that Tripod's tail got caught in the door causing the poor dog to yelp with pain. Tripod hobbled away from the house, pausing momentarily to lick his tail. An eerie feeling crept over Farmer Johnson as he scanned the night sky and saw the light in the distance. He strode out into the wheat field looking for the source of the light. Tripod hopped along beside him, excited to be out on a night walk with his master.

Farmer Johnson paused thinking he had heard a sound, changed direction, and picked up his pace. He snuck up to the spot where he thought he had heard a noise only to find a cow staring blankly back at him and chewing its cud. The cow froze mid-bite looking puzzled as the farmer shone his flashlight into its face. Farmer Johnson caught his breath, exhaled with relief, and then pushed onward.

# ⊙⊙⊙

## JOHNSON WHEAT FIELD
## NEBRASKA, UNITED STATES
## PLANET EARTH

Gilbert had almost reached the light source. He emerged from a thicket of wheat to find himself in a strange depression where the wheat had been flattened down as if trampled, yet none of the stalks were broken — they were merely bent over at the base. The hair on the back of Gilbert's neck began to tingle. He had the distinct sense that he was being watched. An owl hooted in the distance, momentarily distracting him. He accidentally backed into someone right behind him. He tripped and fell on top of the sitting stranger, and they rolled around on the ground.

*"Oh!"* Gilbert screamed.

*"Ieeee!"* shrieked a girl's voice.

Gilbert and the girl stared at each other for a second in disbelief, then both quickly scampered backwards. His pulse quickened. They stared silently at each other for several moments. As Gilbert's eyes adjusted to the darkness, he began to notice details about this mysterious girl that were not apparent to him before. This girl had oversized blue eyes that seemed to peer right into the depths of his soul, turquoise skin that shone in the moonlight and, even stranger, she had two tiny antennae that stemmed from either side of her head.

Gilbert froze, not knowing how to react. After a moment had passed, he realized that he wasn't in immediate mortal danger. He finally gathered up enough courage to speak.

"Wh-wh-who are you?" A brief moment of silence passed, punctuated by the sound of crickets.

"Wh-who are you?" he stuttered again. Another interval of silence passed as they stared at each other. Gilbert saw that the mysterious girl was dressed in some kind of shimmering outfit, and her large, bright, blue eyes glowed in the moonlight like sapphires.

"You Terran?" the girl inquired in a voice that mirrored Gilbert's quivering tone.

"I am a b-boy…uh, a human…a boy…a human boy. G-G-Gilbert is my name."

"Hu-mon…b-boy? I am Aoléon," she said, clumsily mimicking his stuttered response; although, she did not seem the least bit afraid.

Gilbert let out a nervous laugh. "Ae-oh-lee-uhn?" he quivered, sounding out each syllable of her name.

"Yes," the girl nodded and smiled.

"Did you come from up there?" Gilbert motioned toward the sky.

"You know that I come?" Aoléon asked as she peered deeper into Gilbert's eyes. And in that instant, all of his memories since early childhood flooded through his mind — thousands of overlapping images all playing at once. The images went by so fast that he could barely keep up. He began to panic as he realized that this girl was somehow able to view all of his thoughts and memories like someone watching a movie in fast-forward. He suddenly felt totally exposed and vulnerable. Aoléon's expression shifted, the flood of images immediately stopped, and an overwhelming calm fell over Gilbert, setting him at ease.

"No…uh…there were strange dreams…but…I had no idea…Well, I did sense something. You're not…human are you? Where did you come from?" Gilbert asked, mustering his courage.

"The fourth planet — the red planet with two half-moons," Aoléon responded. She made an arching motion with her finger and drew an outline of a circle in the air over her head against the backdrop of the starry night sky. A glow appeared and for a moment, everything seemed to slow. Where the wheat field had been just a moment before, stars now appeared. A planet formed, and Gilbert and Aoléon orbited around it as if they were flying through space. He realized this was some kind of holographic image being projected into his brain, but it felt as if he were really there, actually orbiting the planet. As he gazed at the glowing red planet, he recognized it as one that he had seen hundreds of times through his telescope. With a flash, the hologram disappeared, and he was back in the wheat field.

"Mars! You must have come from Mars!" Gilbert cried with an expression of amazement and wonder. He gazed into Aoléon's deep blue eyes that sparkled in the moonlight.

"It is so," she said. The corner of her mouth lifted in a half smile.

Gilbert's mind raced to keep up. His mind flashed through countless thoughts and images as things began to register with him. *She's an alien — a Martian! I am speaking to a Martian! This is so cool!* he thought. Aoléon smiled in acknowledgment as if she were somehow sharing all his thoughts.

"Indeed. It is 'so cool' to meet you, too," replied Aoléon.

"How can we understand each other…I mean, how is that possible?" Gilbert gasped, trying to keep his wits about him. He continued to stare at her in disbelief. "Am I dreaming?"

"I think, and you understand. You think, and I understand. You feel, and I feel. Understand?" Aoléon smiled at him, making Gilbert feel more at ease. He could barely concentrate on what she was saying to him.

*Can she really read my mind?* Gilbert thought, staring at her. She nodded. "Wow…so cool! Do you have any other powers?" Feeling a bit more at ease, he spoke with greater confidence.

"Pow…ers?" she croaked, crossing her legs and stretching her back upwards so that she was now sitting in front of him with near-perfect posture. Again, he noticed her striking blue eyes.

"Yes — like can you fly, or levitate a rock, or shoot a laser beam?"

"Think not," she giggled.

"I always wanted to go into space," he beamed.

"Some say Terrans are a contagious disease. Are you contagious?" She scooted away from Gilbert a little.

Gilbert coughed once as if to prove to himself that he wasn't ill. "I had the chickenpox once, but I'm fine now."

"Ooh, that is good. But, I am not sure you would like it on Mars. Terra is a much nicer place. Lots of fresh air and green vegi-tables."

"You mean trees?" Gilbert chuckled.

"Just so," she said smiling at him. "Learning alien languages does not come easily for me, but in time I will be better. The more time with you, the more I learn."

"Are you kidding? You're amazing!"

By now he was relaxed, and Gilbert finally took a long good look at his companion. Aoléon was short, about four feet eight inches high, but Gilbert was not much taller. She was somewhat lanky with slender legs and arms proportional to her body. He realized that the two antennae on her head were *not* antennae as he had first thought because he could now see tiny humid air puffs coming from them as she breathed.

Off in the distance they heard a dog barking. "Uh oh, we've got to get out of here fast! That must be Farmer Johnson and his mean old three-legged hound dog."

"Time to go to the ship."

### ⊙⊙⊙

Having discovered a scent to follow, Tripod kept trying to run but was having difficulty. He quickly hobbled up and over a nearby hill and tumbled down the other side, unable to control his descent with his single front leg. Now on level terrain, the hound pushed through the tall stalks of wheat like a bumbling torpedo and headed toward Gilbert, Aoléon and her ship. Farmer Johnson tried desperately to keep up with him and mumbled curses under his breath as he ran.

Tripod lost his footing and fell onto the ground. Farmer Johnson tripped over him, and they both tumbled over each other, landing in a cow patty. Tripod caught a strong scent that wasn't from the cow dung — but from Gilbert who had recently passed this way. Quickly getting up, Tripod took off after Aoléon and Gilbert while Farmer Johnson took his time and wiped himself off before continuing on at a slower pace.

When Tripod finally caught up with Aoléon and Gilbert, he started to bark with excitement. Aoléon led Gilbert by the hand, occasionally stumbling over the odd gopher hole. They ran as fast as they could toward the saucer. The hound hopped after them, falling to the ground and quickly bounding back up to continue pursuit.

As they approached the saucer's landing spot in the nearby crop circle, Tripod fell into a deep gopher hole. The dog yelped and whimpered in agony, unable to continue. Hearing the dog's cries, Aoléon stopped to look back. Gilbert slid to a halt, as well.

"I sense great pain. Must help."

"Tripod must have tripped in one of those gopher holes," Gilbert wheezed, trying to catch his breath.

"I must look…must go back to help," Aoléon responded as she gazed back toward the spot where Tripod had fallen and now lay unmoving.

"Don't be silly. Come on — let's go. Farmer Johnson is getting closer," urged Gilbert while gently tugging on Aoléon's arm.

"Great pain. It needs our help," Aoléon protested turning back toward Tripod.

"Oh all right, but we need to be quick. If Farmer Johnson catches us we could be...well, he doesn't like it when people trespass on his farm."

Aoléon and Gilbert doubled back toward where they heard the dog howling. In the deep gopher hole, Tripod lay shaking, his leg still trapped.

"Looks like a broken leg," Gilbert said as he examined the poor creature. Aoléon bent over to get a closer look at it. The dog slowly lifted up his eyes to them and let out a whimper. Aoléon stretched out her arm and lightly touched the dog's forehead with her gloved fingers. A glowing blue light emanated from her hand and slowly expanded outward enveloping Tripod in a halo of pulsating light. Her touch seemed to ease the dog's pain, and he relaxed as Gilbert watched, amazed. Aoléon and Gilbert gently lifted the dog out of the gopher hole and laid him on the ground. They examined the dog and his broken leg.

Aoléon touched Tripod's leg, and the bones magically seemed to heal themselves. "Better now," Aoléon said, relieved.

"How did you...? What the...Th-Th-"

"That," Aoléon helped him.

Gilbert nodded emphatically. "That was incredible!"

"Not really. I create isomorphic projection of animal body using temporal displacement field to make an earlier form to heal his current form. The creature healed himself... with my help."

Gilbert looked puzzled, but before he could ask another question he heard a noise, which diverted his attention. Farmer Johnson came into view and fired a warning shot into the air. "Trespassers! Vandals! Stop! I'll get you!" Farmer Johnson shouted, shaking his shotgun at them.

Gilbert's heart skipped a beat. "Come on!" Not recognizing Gilbert, and seeing only darkened forms that he thought were vandals, Farmer Johnson took aim with his shotgun and pulled the trigger. "No!" Gilbert screamed, just as he heard the shot from the gun. Aoléon raised her arms and extended her fingers, exposing her gloved palms; bubbles of energy shot out from her hands. As if in slow motion, the buckshot stopped just before hitting Gilbert in the chest and fell harmlessly to the ground. Farmer Johnson's jaw dropped, and he stood motionless, suffering from a momentary lapse of reason — his brain unable to comprehend what his eyes just beheld.

"Come!" urged Aoléon, taking Gilbert by the hand and pulling him along as she ran. Gilbert's mind floated somewhere above the scene looking down on himself, watching as they ran together through the field. Elvis had left the building. His lights were on, but nobody was home.

They sprinted as quickly as they could to Aoléon's saucer, which appeared to be a seamless, spherical, metallic object. As far as Gilbert could see, it had no doors and no windows.

"Er, how do we get inside?"

"Watch," Aoléon said as she waved her arm causing part of the side of the ship to dematerialize. It resembled heat rising from a road on a hot summer day. The metal vaporized to reveal a portal entrance, which led into the saucer. Gilbert hesitated for a moment before he passed through the phased ship hull. They clambered inside and took their seats. Farmer Johnson trailed behind them, closing fast, but he stopped short when the saucer came into view.

"It is not magic. I simply phase-shifted that section of the hull to the post-plasma beam manifestation to form the portal opening," Aoléon replied, smiling.

"Uhh, right," Gilbert responded, not having a clue what she meant. Then he realized she had responded to a question that had just popped into his mind, but he had never actually asked it out loud.

Aoléon closed the opening to the saucer and waved her hand in front of the main console, bringing the ship to life. Gilbert noticed that the inside of the ship was surprisingly spartan. Everything was smooth, curved, and seamlessly connected. It possessed few distinguishing features as if the entire ship, including the cockpit, had been molded out of a single piece of metal.

Gilbert turned around and touched a spherical object positioned behind him that was no larger than a basketball. "What's this round thing for?"

"That is the fusion core," Aoléon replied. Gilbert gasped and snatched his hand back. Suddenly the ship powered down.

"Did I do that?"

"The flux capacitor has been on the fritz."

"Really?"

"No silly, only teasing. Thankfully my saucer is much more durable than one of your 'Deloreans.'" She giggled. The ship powered up again. Lights appeared forming into balls of plasma that circled the craft.

"How did you know about that?!"

"I saw it in your mind," she replied. "This ship could fly right through the corona of a star, and it would not even blemish the hull. You could never break it, even if you tried."

"That's a relief," Gilbert sighed. "Er…How can you navigate?" he inquired looking around at the opaque metallic interior of the craft. "Don't you have windows?"

Aoléon waved her hand over a holographic icon, and the hull of the ship transformed from opaque metal into a semitransparent surface. Gilbert could now see directly through the hull of the saucer itself. "Only primitive spacecraft require windows. They are a structural weakness and completely unnecessary. With my telepathic interlink to the onboard A.I., I can see in any direction I wish outside the ship without having to turn my head."

"A.I.?"

"Artificial Intelligence. Say hello to Gilbert," Aoléon said, speaking to the ship.

"Greetings Terran," spoke a disembodied female voice that just seemed to pop inside his head without making an actual sound. It was as if his brain were linked to the ship, as well.

"SWEET!" Gilbert exclaimed as he looked around through the solid-yet-transparent hull of the ship at the ground below and the sky above sparkling with stars. "Let's roll!"

"I hope you mean that figuratively," Aoléon grinned.

The saucer lurched and came to life with a deep humming sound. The low thrum transitioned into a higher-pitched whirring noise as the saucer's reactor came up to full power. Plasma orbs like tiny colored suns began to appear outside the ship, spinning faster and faster around the hull of the saucer while casting multicolored shadows onto the ground. The cockpit shimmered as lights on the main console sprang to life. Floating transparent images of light and symbols appeared to hover in front of them forming a strange kind of holographic instrument display system.

"What's that?" inquired Gilbert as he reached out with his hand and moved it through a hologram of a strange Martian symbol that hovered above the console in front of him. It wavered slightly as his hand passed through the image, and then a burst of light appeared briefly outside the ship.

"Ieeeee! Do not touch!" cried Aoléon. But it was too late. Gilbert had accidentally caused the ship to fire a blast into the pasture, creating a zero-point energy field around each of the cows. At that moment, all the cows and Tripod gently floated upward, ascending past two birds that peered at them, puzzled. The cows shared frightened glances as they rose skyward, but one continued to chew placidly on a huge tuft of grass.

"Uhh…sorry," Gilbert replied sheepishly.

"Okay. Now we go."

Gilbert turned his head in time to see the cows levitate. "Look! The cows! They're floating!" Gilbert scrunched his nose up against the hull of the saucer in an attempt to get a better look.

"Yes, yes…You have trapped them into a zero-point energy bubble. They will return to the ground unharmed… eventually," she said. "Just try not to touch anything else, please!"

Farmer Johnson reached the edge of the crop circle clearing where the ship sat hovering, just in time to see it ascend straight up about one hundred feet, stop, shoot over his farmhouse, stop, and then disappear in a streak of light, shooting over the horizon. He fumbled with his shotgun to try and get off a shot, but the ship accelerated so fast it was gone before he could raise the gun.

"Sweet Nellie! That was a UFO! What are they doing to my cows?" Tripod, levitating along with the cows, suddenly dropped from the sky and landed on top of Farmer Johnson, knocking him flat on the ground.

# FLYING COWS
## CHAPTER THREE

# MCCONNELL AIR FORCE BASE, WICHITA, KANSAS, UNITED STATES PLANET EARTH

Airman Buzz sat at his post in McConnell Air Force Base in Kansas playing a video game on his smartphone when he heard the signal. The automatic radar-tracking scope registered a new contact. A beeping noise brought the radar controller's attention away from his game. Buzz focused on a white blinking dot that appeared on the radar screen. The radio in the control room crackled to life. "This is NORAD. We are declaring a Fastwalker alert. We are tracking a Fastwalker heading eastbound at twelve hundred knots. Please confirm."

Airman Buzz keyed the com-link and responded. "Copy that, NORAD. This is McConnell. We have the Fastwalker on our scope. Trajectory and speed are remaining constant. We're scrambling fighters to welcome our uninvited guest."

"What is it?" Buzz's commanding officer inquired as he entered the room.

"NORAD declared a Fastwalker alert, Captain," Buzz said.

"You're joking. A Fastwalker?"

"Yes sir, a super-luminal alien spacecraft just entered our atmosphere. NORAD has it at four hundred fifty miles inbound — moving real fast. Whew! Negative IFF Idents. That confirms it ain't one of ours!"

Two F-22 Raptors, the U.S. Air Force's most advanced fighter aircraft, vectored in toward the unknown contact. "Rabid Monkey in pursuit," the first F-22 pilot said into his helmet microphone.

"Missiles now armed. Man! He is movin'!" exclaimed Angry Dog, the other F-22 pilot. The two F-22 Raptors banked while staying in formation with their afterburners exploding full blast. The F-22s accelerated past Mach 2 toward the alien saucer.

☉☉☉

The saucer flew low over farmhouses and wheat fields, blowing shingles off roofs in the process. Gilbert beamed at Aoléon. "Whoo-hoo!" he shouted as the ship made a particularly sharp bank. He was seated in a special chair that had conformed around his body like a cocoon. The ship flew extremely fast, making sharp horizontal and vertical turns. Somehow the ship was able to cancel the immense G-forces and inertia that would have crushed a pilot in a conventional aircraft maneuvering at those speeds. To Gilbert, it barely felt like he was moving at all, and yet, he could clearly see the earth and the clouds rapidly passing him by through the transparent saucer hull.

Aoléon seemed to be controlling the ship without touching any controls. It must be mind control. Aoléon looked over and nodded…then she winked at him. The console projected a holographic display with blue and pink three-dimensional images that shimmered in front of the transparent saucer dome. Tiny beams of light projected their trajectory with cross-hair boxes blinking next to what Gilbert took to be more Martian hieroglyphs.

ල ල ල

Meanwhile Angry Dog, the lead F-22 Raptor pilot, checked the heads-up display inside his cockpit as the radar-tracking symbol blinked, locking onto the alien saucer.

A computerized female voice spoke in calm, even tones, indicating that he was now ready to fire. The pilot shifted his thumb up the side of his joystick, and his index finger found the missile launch button.

He spoke rapidly, holding his finger over the button. "NORAD, this is Angry Dog interceptor flight from McConnell. We have an unidentified flying object in our sights. I repeat…we have an unidentified flying object not responding to our hails. Requesting permission to fire."

"Roger that, Angry Dog. The National Command Authority has granted you permission to fire. Weapons hot. Fire at will," responded NORAD.

"Tally ho!" Angry Dog's gloved hand flexed, tightening his grip on the joystick as he prepared to fire, when he noticed something unusual floating toward his canopy — a cow, which he was about to overtake at Mach 2.

"NORAD — uh — we have cows, sir!"

"Please repeat," NORAD responded.

"Cows! Flying cows!"

That instant, the lead jet roared past a floating cow. "Moooo!" exclaimed the cow. Angry Dog watched as it quickly disappeared from view. He then faced forward just in time to see another cow flying directly at him. It slammed into his cockpit with tremendous force, bounced off the plane and spun away unharmed, protected by the zero-point energy field surrounding it. The plane buffeted a bit upon impact, but Angry Dog quickly regained control of the jet, angled the plane back toward the saucer and squeezed the fire button. The missile bay doors of the F-22 Raptor snapped opened. Two missiles dropped from the plane and rocketed toward the alien spacecraft.

ⓞⓞⓞ

Aoléon grimaced as the telepathic link between her and the ship warned her of the fast-approaching missiles.

"We're in trouble! It's the U.S. Air Force!" Gilbert proclaimed as he glanced back over his shoulder at the oncoming plumes of smoke, realizing that these were inbound missiles heading right for them.

"Their primitive craft cannot harm us," Aoléon responded calmly as she swerved and banked the saucer making several abrupt, ninety-degree changes in direction, easily evading the missiles.

"You're sure about that?" said Gilbert, eyeing Aoléon doubtfully.

☉☉☉

A passenger plane flew by on its way to Chicago, and a young boy gazed out from his window seat, daydreaming. He noticed two tiny specks: one looked like a shooting star and the other like a plane moving quickly and growing larger. "Hey, Mom," he said tugging on his mother's sleeve. "Something's happening outside the plane."

"Shhh. Not now. Trying to read," responded the boy's mother. She turned the page of her magazine, *Mothering for Mothers*, and kept reading, not even looking at her son.

The saucer and the two F-22 Raptors hurtled past the passenger plane so quickly that the boy could feel the shock waves vibrating his whole body. A bright flash of light followed by a loud rushing sound and a sonic boom buffeted the plane. The frightened passengers in the main cabin jumped in their seats. The passenger plane took a sharp dive as the pilots struggled to regain control.

"Mallard Air Flight 242 heavy is declaring an emergency...Mayday! Mayday!" radioed the pilot as the plane took a nosedive for the ground. The lights to the *Fasten Seatbelt* sign suddenly turned on, but it was too late. The plane already was in a dive, and passengers were being tossed everywhere.

"Ahhh! What's going on?" the boy's mother screamed in panic, dropping her magazine. Other screams could be heard throughout the plane. The pilots steadied the plane, and the passengers regained their composure, exchanging quizzical looks. One woman who had been in the process of putting on makeup was caught off guard by the sudden turbulence and accidentally spread lipstick all over her face. She peered at herself in her cosmetic mirror, shrieked again, and quickly tried to rub it off with a tissue. Several people seated nearby coughed loudly, trying to suppress their laughter.

"Wow, that was COOL!" the boy exclaimed with a giddy laugh.

ʘ ʘ ʘ

The saucer came to an instantaneous stop midair. The missiles and the two raptors flew past the now hovering saucer. The two planes banked hard turns to try to come around again, but before they could complete their turns, the ship quickly accelerated and shot past them. The F-22 lead pilot watched the saucer rapidly accelerate and pull away from him as if he were standing still. It became obvious to the pilots that their jets were simply outclassed by a ship capable of displacing the forces of gravity and inertia. The saucer shot up through the clouds, which swirled around the hull of her ship creating a vortex in its wake. The F-22s engaged afterburners for extra speed to try to keep up, but they were unsuccessful.

"Control, this is Rabid Monkey. The bogey is pulling away fast. Unable to match speed to pursue."

"Copy that. Raptors RTB," replied NORAD. "Nellis, this is NORAD. Launch the Aurora Interceptor."

⦿⦿⦿

The MagLev elevator platform ascended toward the surface carrying the Aurora Interceptor. This wasn't a typical elevator. This was an elevator platform large enough to lift an airplane entirely by electromagnets and without any cables. Various levels of the underground base swept past — large rooms with other secret test planes and large lab complexes came and went. Finally, the ascent stopped, and the massive steel blast-proof vault doors opened.

Lights pierced the darkness from within the giant underground hangar at an ultra-secret Air Force base in southwestern Nevada. A single spotlight shone from above, illuminating the aircraft and creating a black triangular silhouette even when fully lit. A large American flag hung on the wall behind the plane. The hangar itself was not your typical box-shaped thin aluminum-paneled airplane hangar. At ground level, it was a reinforced concrete bunker, aerodynamically shaped like a double wedge with vault-thick steel doors designed to withstand the overpressure from an atomic bomb.

Major Buck Turgidson climbed inside the cockpit of the Aurora, fired its engines, and taxied out to the runway. Buck hit the afterburners, and the Aurora took to the sky with a thunderous roar. Accelerating quickly to Mach 5, the ship streaked into the stratosphere climbing rapidly to 60,000 feet just off the California coastline and flying over Malibu, Point Mugu and the Pacific Ocean where it made a gradual 180-degree turn. Now heading toward the Midwest, Turgidson prepared for suborbital burn.

"Engage aerospikes," he commanded through his helmet microphone, speaking to the onboard computer. The aero-spikes shifted their position, diverting the supersonic intake airflow away from the regular jet engines and into the manifold for the laser pulse-detonation wave engines.

"Engaging aerospikes," a female computerized voice responded, acknowledging the order and telling Turgidson that he could cancel the order, if necessary.

"Going hypersonic," Turgidson commented into his helmet microphone. "Engage," he said as he activated the laser pulse-detonation wave engines.

"Suborbital burn commencing! Please fasten your seat belt and keep your arms and legs inside the vehicle at all times," the female voice responded.

Thrust back into his seat by the abrupt acceleration of the plane, Turgidson's vision blurred momentarily from the immense G-forces. The Aurora shot upward like a rocket, going faster and faster. A donuts-on-a-rope contrail emerged from the pulse-detonation wave engines as the plane accelerated past Mach 8. Reaching its apogee on the edge of space, the Aurora arced back toward Earth. Turgidson's vision cleared long enough to see the curvature of the Earth spread out before him. The blackness of space now surrounded him, but below he could see the entire North American continent. He glanced down at his altimeter that showed he was eighty miles above the surface of the Earth.

Now flying faster than Mach 12, the computerized navigation system linked into the NORAD GPS satellite navigational system and vectored his plane to intercept the

UFO. Reentering the Earth's atmosphere like a ballistic missile somewhere over midwestern Canada, Turgidson caught up to the alien craft over East Pen Island on the south end of Hudson's Bay.

☉☉☉

Gilbert glanced back and saw the USAF jet trailing close behind them. "Aoléon, they're back!" In response, Aoléon turned north, flying over parts of the Canadian Arctic and the Atlantic Ocean where she then headed toward the North Pole.

"Hold on. This much fun."

"Fun? Are you kidding me? This is crazy!" Gilbert shrieked.

Aoléon giggled. "How do Terrans say…like taking sweet from neonatal sub-unit?"

"Neo *what?!* Oh, you mean *candy*…from a *baby!*" Gilbert choked. A frantic pursuit ensued. The chase led them over snow-capped mountains, through gullies and over fields as they headed north toward Canada's Arctic tundra region and the North Pole.

ତତତ

The Aurora's incredible speed this low to the ground created a giant shock wave vortex behind the plane, knocking fully grown pine trees completely over while generating huge avalanches of snow in its wake. This was business as usual for the ace test pilot who had participated in UFO chase missions before. Major Turgidson fired his particle beam cannon in short bursts at the saucer but kept missing.

ତତତ

Aoléon's saucer had far greater maneuverability and easily avoided the incoming fire. Gilbert, however, became unnerved by the blasts of laser-cannon fire streaking past their ship. His knuckles turned white as he tightened his grip on the sides of his seat.

Aoléon sensed Gilbert's unease. "The primitive particle weapon cannot harm us."

ⓞⓞⓞ

Vistas of sparkling ocean sailed past the saucer in a blur, dashed with the occasional iceberg as they flew from Crown Prince Frederik Island over Baffin Bay toward Melville Bugt, Greenland. A massive rooster-tail explosion of water chased the Aurora Interceptor as it rocketed after them. They flew low over two fishing trawlers, which were swamped by the spray caused by the shockwave of the Aurora. One boat almost capsized, and two crew members were thrown overboard.

Leaving the ocean, they sped over land, flying up and over craggy ice-cliff peaks flecked with dark blue ice granules the size of buses, followed by a long plateau of snow and ice and the occasional snow-covered mountain. The saucer darted around sharp corners, through deep fragmented canyons of white snow and ice, over snowfields and large glaciers — all with the jet in hot pursuit.

☉ ☉ ☉

Bursts of laser fire streaked past Aoléon's saucer, narrowly missing it and exploding into the snowy canyon walls. "Ahhh, that was close!" said Gilbert as part of the snow-covered canyon was struck by fire, and large chunks of ice and snow fell, barely missing their ship.

While Gilbert was holding on for dear life, Aoléon giggled with pleasure as she played chase with the USAF pilot. She began to hum a strange tune. "Ou, alay, ali, alou, da di, da da, da doo," she hummed to herself while Gilbert just stared at her, wide-eyed.

*I've been abducted by a nutty alien who's a speed freak!* Gilbert thought, trying to calm himself. Aoléon simply smiled and kept humming her tune.

Careening south from the North Pole, they flew over Greenland and Iceland. They barely missed colliding with the ice-capped peaks of the Vatnajökull Mountains. Shooting southward over the North Atlantic, the saucer skimmed the surface just a few hundred feet off the water. In short order, the spacecraft reached the British Isles, flew over Belfast, Ireland and then continued southward toward London with the Aurora in close pursuit.

ಠಠಠ

Overlooking Big Ben and Parliament from the opposite side of the River Thames, a husband and wife were enjoying a picnic. The husband picked up a piece of chicken and was taking a bite when his wife stopped him short. "Dahling, do you think you could possibly use your utensils? We're not cannibals, you know," squeaked Patsy McClellan as she carefully spread out her pressed silk napkin on her lap.

"Uh, yes, my dear Patsy. I was actually planning on…"

Without warning, a streak of light appeared in the sky. Mr. McClellan started to speak and then paused mid-sentence to watch, forgetting the conversation he was having with his wife. The saucer and the USAF plane darted overhead followed by a tremendous sonic boom thunderclap that echoed off the buildings of Parliament and shook the ground. Dozens of windows in the nearby buildings shattered, and car alarms chirped as the shock wave from the Aurora struck them.

Patsy screamed, spilling her tea onto her husband's lap. Mr. McClellan jumped up and let out a yelp of pain while grabbing at his burning midsection. A chicken leg flew up in the air from his lunch plate, bounced off his wife's head and landed in her now partially empty teacup.

ⓒⓒⓒ

"Target locked. Fox One away," Buck Turgidson gasped, finally having a clear shot at the saucer. The missile launched from the Aurora Interceptor sped off toward the saucer.

ⓒⓒⓒ

Again, the saucer automatically detected the inbound missile and warned Aoléon of a collision via telepathic link. Just then on the holographic view screen, Aoléon's mother, Phobos, appeared and asked her what she was doing and why she was not yet home for dinner.

"I know. I know. I am busy," Aoléon responded briskly.

"You know, you shouldn't talk on the phone while driving," interjected Gilbert nervously.

"Who was that? Aoléon, are you harassing the Terrans again?"

"No mother. Just getting in a little practice before my pilot's exam. See you soon."

*PRACTICE?! Oh, my, gosh! We're gonna die!* thought Gilbert.

"No worries. I have been practicing for whole week now…we will be fine. Trust Aoléon!" she said to Gilbert, bobbing her head up and down with a large grin.

"I'm dead," Gilbert whispered to himself.

"Aoléon, please come home immediately, or you will be late for evening consumption."

"Affirmative, mother," Aoléon said calmly as the com-link went dead.

"Uhh…watch those cliffs!" cried Gilbert.

Aoléon, momentarily distracted by Gilbert, swerved the saucer a little bit clumsily and had to correct her trajectory causing the ship to nip the ocean's surface. Water shot up around the hull of the craft, but surprisingly the craft didn't lurch. She banked the saucer, just barely missing the craggy cliffs that had appeared out of the fog that adorned the rocky shore of northern France. Gilbert sighed with relief as they barely missed the cliffs but tensed up again as Aoléon flew low to the ground; he wondered whether he was going to survive the trip.

They had reached the center of Paris, and Aoléon's saucer flew through the famous Arc de Triomphe and down the Champs-Élysées, the main street. Cars along the street screeched to a halt as Aoléon's flying saucer and the Aurora flew directly over their heads, the reverberations from the sonic boom setting off car alarms and breaking shop windows as they went.

The pursuing USAF plane fired again. The missile was close behind them now and was about to intercept their ship when Aoléon gave the telepathic command to change direction, shooting the saucer suddenly skywards. The ship made a near ninety-degree vertical turn without slowing down just as Aoléon and Gilbert were about to collide with a giant Ferris wheel called La Grande Roue de Paris on the Champs-Élysées near some famous landmarks — the American Embassy, a museum called Le Musée du Louvre, and Le Jardin des Tuileries, a magical garden.

The missile overshot them and impacted with the giant Ferris wheel, causing an explosion, knocking it off its posts, and sending it rolling down the street. Aoléon responded quickly by accelerating even more rapidly. Her ship climbed vertically at an incredible rate toward space.

ⓞⓞⓞ

*"Zut alors!"* exclaimed a Frenchman as he watched the giant burning Ferris wheel roll down the Champs-Élysées.

ⓞⓞⓞ

"Inbound bogey has accelerated past ten thousand miles per hour and changed its vector, heading for space," announced Turgidson.

"Copy that. Pursue as long as possible," NORAD replied.

"Roger. Bogey going vertical. Pursuing," Turgidson announced. The McConnell radar operator was momentarily confused until he realized the pilot was referring to the UFO and not some other kind of unidentified object.

The saucer ascended through the clouds toward space. In a last-ditch effort, Turgidson fired his only remaining missile. In less than a tenth of a second, Aoléon's saucer increased its vertical climb speed from Mach 5 to about 350 times the speed of sound — roughly 250,000 miles per hour. The saucer shot out of the Earth's atmosphere and into space in less than a second. To Major Turgidson's eyes, the ship accelerated so fast that it seemed to vanish in front of him. Unable to track the ship any longer, the missile instead searched for a new target and circled back toward the Aurora Interceptor and Major Turgidson.

"Uh, oh…*Mommy!*" Turgidson cried out, realizing he was on a collision course with his own missile. He ejected just before the missile collided with the Aurora. As he fell back to Earth in his ejection seat, the plane exploded in a giant fireball. He plummeted to Earth at an alarming rate. At the last moment, his parachute opened. He slammed into his harness and began to float slowly downward over Paris.

Turgidson sighed with relief thinking he was finally safe when he noticed that he was coming uncomfortably close to La Tour Eiffel with no way to avoid it. His fall came to an abrupt halt as his parachute caught on the tip of the famous Paris landmark. People stared up in disbelief at the man hanging from a parachute while tourists snapped photos and debris from the plane rained down around them.

ⓞⓞⓞ

The stars streaked by as Aoléon's saucer accelerated past light speed. Almost instantly, the saucer slowed, and the

planet Mars came into view. Her saucer shot past Phobos, one of Mars' two small moons and headed toward the dark side of Mars before descending through the Martian atmosphere toward Olympus Mons — the largest known shield volcano in the solar system.

# SITUATION ROOM

## CHAPTER FOUR

# SITUATION ROOM
# THE WHITE HOUSE, WASHINGTON, D.C.
# UNITED STATES, PLANET EARTH

The Secretary of Defense, General Stryker who was Chairman of the Joint Chiefs of Staff (CJCS), the Vice President, and the White House Chief of Staff were sitting around a large table in the Situation Room located in a bunker beneath the White House. The Secretary of Defense, Engelbert Humperdinck III — no relation to the famous German composer, nor to any prince or princess, nor to anyone else you might know — but he probably *wished* it were the case. Suffice it to say, like most politicians, he was really good at making things up while projecting an overly inflated self-image.

Secretary of Defense Humperdinck was a tall, skinny man with a bald head so large and perfectly round that a NASA astronomer might mistake it for a small planetoid. He wore a handmade dark grey pinstripe suit, a white shirt with a baby blue tie, and a pair of shiny, black, wingtip shoes.

General Stryker, chairman of the CJCS, wore the uniform of a four-star general. A sharp jawline and broad shoulders of an American football linebacker gave him a commanding presence. Although in his old age, he had grown a bit plump around the midsection. His features were amplified by an overbearing personality and a deep booming voice. "Mr. President," General Stryker greeted the President who had just entered the room.

The President, of tall and slender build with slightly greying hair, walked into the room wearing his bathrobe and white fluffy bunny feet slippers. The others in the room greeted the President while trying not to stare at his slippers.

"Russ, we have a situation in Nebraska, and we just lost one of our Aurora-class planes over Paris," reported Vice President Richard Tator.

The President glanced up at the sign over the door that said "SITUATION ROOM." He wore a confused expression. "What is it?" inquired President Russell Sumach.

"It's the capital of France, sir," said Vice President Richard Tator.

"No, I mean what's this room? I haven't been here before, have I? Never mind — proceed. I'm just going to get some coffee first," said the President as he lumbered over to a coffee dispenser and started pouring himself a cup.

The Air Force advisor tried to brief the President on the pursuit of the alien flying saucer; however, the President wasn't paying attention. As he picked up his cup of coffee and walked back to the head of the table, the President accidentally caught his bathrobe on the back of a chair, yanking it off him. The President, realizing that he was standing in front of all his advisors wearing nothing but his underwear and slippers, turned pink with embarrassment while his staff simply stared in awe at the Presidential Seal on his briefs.

"My kids have a pair just like that," said an aide, motioning toward the President's fluffy bunny feet. She quickly realized that she shouldn't have said a word because everyone else tried to suppress their laughter.

The President quickly grabbed his bathrobe and covered himself. "Never mind. Continue," said the President acting as if nothing had happened.

The presidential advisor coughed, trying not to laugh; whereas the Secretary of Defense just glared. "Right," he said as if choking. "The Air Force is currently in pursuit of a Fastwalker — what we think is an interplanetary UFO. We have been tracking it for the last few minutes over the midwestern United States. We believe it was making crop circles, sir. There are currently some reports of it on the news."

The President motioned for them to turn on the TV. A news anchor for CRN, a leading news network, appeared on the screen. "And now to Harry Knittle, our correspondent at NASA. Harry—" said the news anchorman. The President, who had picked up the TV remote, changed the channel to a cartoon station. The advisor quickly took the remote from him, changing the channel back while giving the President a stern look. The presidential expression reflected disappointment as the news came back on.

"This is Harry Knittle with CRN reporting from Cape Canaveral, NASA. Sumach from Mars? NASA scientists confirmed today that the eroded remains of the Alba Patera crater on Mars precisely match the face of President Russell Sumach."

One scientist, Dr. Gene Poule, had spectacles with particularly thick lenses that magnified the light, making his eyes appear to bulge. He exclaimed in a tinny voice: "It's him! There's his nose...that ridge, see? And see the crater rim marking his receding hairline? His hair appears in this region's valley." The President looked sideways at the screen, then turned to look at his reflection in the table next to him, stroked his hair, and smiled at himself as if noticing his own stunning good looks for the first time.

"The White House had no comment," announced reporter Harry Knittle.

"Those guys *never* have anything to say," said the President. "Receding hairline…Humpf! What do they know?!"

"Russ, ignore them. You don't have a receding hairline," said Vice President Tator.

The news broadcast continued its report. "However, Grouse McNoggin, president of EA — Enemies of Aliens — told CRN: 'It's the same kind of fool who built the Titanic and labeled it unsinkable that proclaims we are alone in the universe and never have been visited. Oh, the hubris! This is the evidence we have been looking for!' Now back to you," said Harry Knittle.

The President quickly changed the channel again. An insurance commercial came on the TV. A disembodied announcer was speaking: "Are you worried about aliens invading your home in the middle of the night? Well, don't worry anymore. With Better-Life Alien Abduction Insurance, we can give you peace of mind…"

The presidential aide switched the channel back to the news. "This just in: we are getting reports of an unidentified flying object over the midwestern United States. There also have been some recent reports of strange crop circles near the sighting. We are going to our reporter on the scene, Anna Graham, with this hot-breaking story. Anna, over to you," announced the news anchor.

"We're currently at the Johnson farm in central Nebraska where the first sighting occurred. Mr. Johnson was reportedly sleeping in his bedroom when blinding lights from what he claims to be a flying saucer awoke him. Mr. Johnson, would you care to comment on what you saw?" asked the news correspondent.

"Uh, yes I would. I was in my bed when I saw a blindin' light, which lit up my bedroom…"

Mrs. Johnson leaned in front of the camera, cutting off Farmer Johnson mid-sentence. "A stampede of elephants couldn't wake you up! You were comatose and snorin' like a hog. If it wasn't for me, you would have slept through the whole thing!"

"Yes, hun. Well, then everythin' went strangely quiet. I went lookin' out over yonder when I saw it fly over my head faster than a rocket. Then *pfffft!* Gone! It vanished over the horizon," Farmer Johnson said in a self-important tone of voice.

"Amazing. What else did you see?" inquired correspondent Anna Graham.

"My wife wanted me to go outside to have a look-see. So I *went*…you know…to take a look aroun'. I thought I saw two of them varmints skedaddlin' through my field. I fired a couple a warnin' shots, but they got away. My dog is gettin' a little slow in his old age. And he, well, tripped in a gopher hole." Farmer Johnson paused and looked up at the sky as if he were pondering a deep thought. "Somethin' tells me that this wasn't the first time I've come in contact with these things. Every once in a while when I see strange lights in the sky, I blank out, and the next day I have a really sore feelin' on my backside."

"Ah, umm, hmm, that's very interesting. Thank you Mr. Johnson. We now have a special report from Frank, the weatherman," said Anna Graham. Frank, a short, skinny, slightly balding man wearing a dark blue suit was holding a microphone while standing in the center of what appeared to be a crop circle.

"The ancients revered wheat as a sacred plant symbolizing fertility and renewal. Seeds from the 'bread of life' offered new life in abundance and, symbolically, 'sheaves of corn' came to symbolize fertility. The ancients believed that if you were to break a wheat stalk, it would be interpreted as the 'breaking of spirit.' Interestingly, the circles that appear in our fields also appear to demonstrate that symbolic gesture. For when the circle-makers come, they gently bend over the stalks of wheat so that the wheat continues to grow," said Frank gazing up toward the camera and to the night sky beyond.

Frank continued his report looking up at the camera as it craned higher while remaining focused on him. Now high above the ground, the camera continued its pull backward, revealing more and more of the crop circle formation below with the now-tiny commentator standing in its center. "For thousands of years, agriculture has played an important part in world culture. From a religious aspect, there are numerous sowing and harvesting metaphors found within the Bible. 'Separating the wheat from the chaff' is just one such metaphor that the Bible speaks of regarding the forthcoming Messiah. For it would be He that would clear the threshing floor, gather his wheat, or followers, into the barn and burn the remaining chaff with unquenchable fire!"

Just then Frank heard a "Moooooo" sound and looked up in time to see a cow fall out of the sky and land on his head, squishing him flat. The camera went black for a moment as the news crew scrambled to cut from that scene. The program returned to the anchor desk.

"We seem to have lost contact with Frank. We now have a report that government agents are arriving on the scene," reported the anchor. Just as the newscaster finished her statement, the program switched to a live camera feed from the Johnson farm. A black stealth VTOL aircraft flew into view and hovered above them, kicking up a small tornado of dust while eight MJ-12 commandos slid down two fast-ropes to the ground in one sweeping motion. They rushed at the group of reporters and bystanders yelling at them to get on the ground quickly. One person resisted. Electric sparks flew from one of the commandos like a Tesla coil and hit the man, knocking him unconscious.

After they had all the "prisoners" facedown on the ground, the team of commandos yelled "CLEAR."

The team leader activated his throat microphone and quietly began to communicate with another member of his team. "SNAKE to BAD KARMA," growled the lead MJ-12 commando.

☉☉☉

About half a mile away, a clump of wheat on the ground barely moved. The end of a 50-caliber sniper rifle peeked out from a wheat clump that comprised part of the sniper's ghillie suit. The sniper peered through his thermal and infrared night vision scope, examining the scene. "Bad Karma here," whispered the sniper into his throat microphone.

"SITREP," commanded Snake, the leader of the commando force, looking for an update.

"No hostiles visible. All civilians accounted for. Clear," replied Bad Karma.

All the civilian bystanders now lay facedown on the ground with their hands flexi-cuffed behind their backs. They peered up at the commandos standing guard over them. Two black vans and one circa-1980s black Ford Crown Victoria sedan (in pristine condition) pulled up to the scene. Two government agents got out of the Crown Vic — one dressed in an all-black suit and the other dressed in an all-white suit. Both were wearing dark black sunglasses, even though it was still nighttime. Out of the black van, streamed more agents in silver biochemical spacesuits carrying small Geiger counters for measuring radioactivity. Others had small LED flashlights mounted onto their helmets and were carrying futuristic-looking hand-held devices that beeped and hummed as they poked and prodded the people on the ground.

Günter, one of the GSG-9 commandos on an MJ-12 exchange program suddenly spoke. "Dat landing jigglez mien strudel." The prisoners who didn't have their faces in the dirt looked up quizzically at him. Without pause, the commando proceeded to remove a piece of apple strudel from his chest pocket and took a bite. Günter looked at them for a second, glanced back at his strudel, and motioned with it toward them. "Vould zu like zome ztrudel? I hav lotz u know." Günter spoke with his mouth full of strudel, his words muffled and slurred. A woman on the ground sighed and fainted just before the camera feed went black.

"Since when do we have Germans in the U.S. Army?" one man asked.

"Shut up!" another commando said as he slapped the man on the side of his head.

"Good evening. This is Agent Black, and I am Agent White. We will be your hosts this evening," one of the government agents spoke, addressing the captured civilians. "This whole area has been officially sealed off and is now a quarantine zone. Everything you have seen or heard here today is now classified top secret under the National Security Act of 1947. You may not discuss anything you have seen or heard here with anyone — not even with your families or spouses. After you have been debriefed, you will have some documents to sign, and then you will be free to go."

"That's just great — a cover up! I always knew the government was hushing this up," muttered one man on the ground.

# MARTIAN MEGALOPOLIS
## CHAPTER FIVE

# SPACE, ABOVE PLANET MARS

Aoléon's saucer dropped out of hyperspace and slowed as Mars came into view. The saucer sped past one of two Martian moons: Phobos, which resembled a thirteen-mile-long heavily pockmarked potato, and Deimos. It then headed around the dark side of the planet.

"Welcome to Mars," Aoléon said as they hovered briefly with the entire hemisphere in view.

"This…this is just incredible. You know, it has always been my dream to go into space. Here I am…hovering over Mars and sitting with a real-life Martian in her ship. The kids at school will never believe it!"

For a brief moment, Gilbert just stared out into space at the giant red planet below. Aoléon watched Gilbert with interest as she read his thoughts. Although Aoléon had seen this sight many times before, it was like seeing it again for the first time through Gilbert's eyes.

"I am glad you like it," Aoléon said, smiling. "Now let me show you my world." She angled the saucer downward through the Martian atmosphere toward the surface of the planet.

Aoléon's saucer descended rapidly from space, entered the Martian atmosphere over the Valles Marineris canyon system and headed northwest toward Olympus Mons. As they approached the volcano, it grew so large it swallowed up everything in sight from horizon to horizon.

"And this is where I live," Aoléon said looking at Gilbert whose eyes had widened with amazement. "This is Olympus Mons, the largest shield volcano in the solar system and my home. Eighty-five thousand feet high, or roughly three times higher than your highest mountain on Terra — the one you call 'Everest.' The base is roughly the size of the place that you call 'Arizona.'"

Aoléon flew her ship down into the caldera — the colossal crater that was situated at the top of the massive volcano. As the ship approached, she communicated with Martian Control. Gilbert was confused as to why they were flying into this seemingly empty caldera that was fifty-three miles long, thirty-eight miles wide and two miles deep — large enough to fit the entire area of Los Angeles County inside with room to spare.

Several bright lights appeared near the craft, darting back and forth like angry fireflies. They kept forming different geometric shapes around the ship when suddenly a beam of light scanned the hull. As the beam passed through the ship, the hull seemed to turn to vapor and become translucent much like waves of heat rising off a road. Except Gilbert felt no heat at all. Suddenly the beam disappeared.

"Sentinel scan. They help guard the airspace around our colony."

Light wavered around the surface of the caldera. Where there first appeared to be Martian sand and rock, a giant force field dome emerged with eight arched obelisk pillars, each more than six miles high. The pillars shimmered and glinted in the setting sun and were made of a bluish metal that created a sharp juxtaposition of color and shape against the heavily oxidized, crimson Martian terrain.

"That's no volcano — it's a space station!"

"Yes, we are definitely not in your Nebraska anymore."

The size of the city overwhelmed Gilbert. "That's not huge…it's…it's…gi-normous!" exclaimed Gilbert as they descended.

Aoléon piloted the ship through the shield gateway and into the Martian megalopolis. Below, thousands of buildings were grouped in several concentric elliptical rings, circles within circles, forming a patchwork pattern that sprawled outward as far as the eye could see. Some buildings stood taller than two miles, and the majority of the city remained hidden deep underground inside the bowels of the massive, extinct volcano, Olympus Mons.

They entered into dense Martian air traffic where swarms of saucers and other flying craft ebbed and flowed in various streams over the giant city like small flies buzzing around a massive fruit bowl. Several ships passed uncomfortably close to them, and Gilbert could see Martians inside the ship who were piloting the craft.

"Why is the city inside a force field dome?" asked Gilbert. There was so much to take in and so many questions bubbling up inside his brain that he felt as if his head might explode from information overload. Gilbert had traveled outside Nebraska just twice in his short lifetime. Once was to go snowboarding in Colorado with his friend's family, and the second time was to go camping with his father in California. Most of Gilbert's life had been spent in Nebraska, a place where the cattle population far exceeded that of the people. It was a place where you could drive for an hour through acres of wheat and corn just to visit your neighbor. Gilbert was now visiting the largest city on Mars — a city so immense that it would dwarf any of the largest cities on Earth — and that overwhelmed him. Not only that, but this particular city happened to be densely populated with beings from an alien race.

"Geotechs constructed the force field dome aeons ago to make protection from sun's powerful rays, to hold atmosphere, and to make defensive shield against hostile attack," replied Aoléon.

"But how did the city just suddenly appear like that?"

"There is a cloaking shield around the city. But also, you Terrans reside in what we call 'third-density phased-matter-state layer' of our bubbleverse, and we Martians primarily reside in fifth-density layer. We just phase-shifted from the third into the fifth-density matter-state layer where you now see our city."

"Look…over there," exclaimed Gilbert pointing outside the portal window. "That building is moving!" Eight colossal panels on the building rotated slowly outward from its center like a flower opening its petals.

This was not a human world like on Earth where everything created fell onto right angles and flat sides. In the megalopolis, everything was organic: curved, smooth and sloping.

As they drew closer, the enormity of these buildings filled him with awe. Some buildings stood more than a kilometer tall and featured giant atriums, landing bays, spires and hallways. All sparkled like jewels set in a giant crown that formed the megalopolis. All the buildings were made of a strange metal that reflected brilliant colors of blue, purple and rusted crimson. The colors shifted with the incidence angle of the sun as their ship flew over the city. It was an amazing sight that was never before beheld by human eyes.

Aoléon's ship approached its designated landing bay where down below crowds of Martians could now be seen walking along moving sidewalks or ambulatories. Some of these walkways climbed vertically up the sides of buildings, and the beings walking on them were somehow able to completely disobey the laws of gravity. In other places, pedestrians could be seen moving upside down along inverted footpaths.

Aoléon docked her ship in one of the many landing bays inside the Martian Intergalactic Spaceport where hundreds of saucers of varying shapes and sizes hovered in place.

Maintenance bots could be seen moving about. Some carried spare parts and equipment to and from the ships, and others conducted repairs. Sparks fell from a plasma-beam fabricator where one of the maintenance bots stood working underneath the hull of a ship not far from where Gilbert stood.

"Here, take my extra spacesuit," Aoléon said as she handed it to him. "Wear it as a disguise. We must sneak you through the Xiocrom security checkpoint. But first, I need to inject you with some harmless nanites."

"You want to inject me with nannies?!"

"No silly, nanites!"

"Is there a problem with your universal translator or something? You're not making any sense."

"They are molecule-sized robotic machines."

"Are you serious?! I'd rather be injected with a nanny!"

Aoléon laughed. "They are integral to your spacesuit. They exist to repair damaged cells, to increase efficiency of your metabolic functions, and to help your lungs break down and process different types of atmospheres. They will live in your body for a short while before you pass them out."

"But how?"

Aoléon tilted her head and whispered in his ear. "You wee them out." She blushed, turning her cheeks darker blue. Aoléon touched a small circular case in the palm of her hand. A tiny tubule snaked out and injected Gilbert with nanites.

"That didn't hurt so bad," Gilbert replied stoically, rubbing the sore spot on his shoulder.

"You should keep the helmet visor closed for the time being to avoid eye contact. And let me put this makeup on you. It will make your skin appear blue like mine!" Aoléon said as she dabbed her makeup over his face. Gilbert shut his eyes and grimaced as she smeared more gunk over his cheeks.

"Okay, but what happens if we get caught?" Gilbert said nasally as Aoléon continued to paint his nose, mashing it flat.

"You do not want to know," Aoléon said, scrunching up her face and becoming suddenly serious. She put away her makeup and looked him over closely. Her face came right next to his, and he stared into her large blue eyes as she inspected her work.

"Wait! Is it like that movie where the aliens suck your brains out with a straw?" Gilbert asked. His eyes wrinkled and his nose crinkled as if he had smelled something foul.

She paused for a moment and peered deeply into Gilbert's eyes, making her go slightly cross-eyed. "Ummmmm…No. Not that bad, but almost," Aoléon said with a half-smile. "No worries. Aoléon will keep you safe." She dabbed some final touches of blue makeup onto his nose.

*Yeah right*, thought Gilbert. *That means a lot, coming from a nutty alien girl who attracts trouble like flies to a cow patty.*

"You tickles me," Aoléon said laughing, her eyes crinkling up in the corners. "There. All done!" she said with a wink. "Here, put this on."

Gilbert took the spacesuit from Aoléon and slid into it. The suit conformed to his body as if it were alive. He felt a strange tingly sensation, like tiny little needles pricking him all over. He shivered.

"Wait, what's happening? It feels like the suit is attaching itself to me or something?"

"Yes, it does that. That sensation you are experiencing is caused by the nano-receivers inside the suit attaching themselves to your muscles and nerve endings."

"But, I don't want any *nano-whatties* attaching themselves to anything of mine! I would like to keep all of my body parts intact! Thank you very much, Miss 'I-don't-care-if-the-U.S.-Air-Force-is-chasing-me-Martian-girl!'"

"Stop fussing. The suit is completely harmless and will react and follow your movement, giving you enhanced strength and speed," Aoléon said as she checked his suit and placed the helmet over his head.

"Forgive me if I don't completely trust your judgment; it's just that I am not used to meeting strange alien girls who get their jollies from making crop circles and playing pranks on the U.S. Air Force."

"We were never in any *real* danger."

"You say!" Gilbert held his breath as if the helmet would cut off his air supply. Aoléon tapped on the helmet, gesturing for him to relax. He finally gasped, taking in a lung full of air. The helmet fed him oxygen, allowing him to breathe. The suit smelled slightly of a flowery perfume that lingered over a stronger smell of almonds and burnt rubber.

"Wait a minute! This suit looks strangely familiar. I think I dreamed about this just the other night!"

"Maybe you have psionic power, too."

"Psionic power? Nah, probably just déjà vu."

Aoléon and Gilbert headed over to the Xiocrom Security Station, a shiny metallic pagoda arching upwards before them. Martian officials eyed Gilbert and Aoléon as they passed through the checkpoint. Arrayed like stanchions on either side of the security checkpoint stood several Martians that were taller than most he had seen — at least so far. Each had a single, large cycloptic eyeball located in the center of his head. The eye seemed to peer right into and through Gilbert as if it were scanning his mind and body.

*If one of those guys had impaired vision they would need some really humongous contact lenses*, thought Gilbert.

"Watchers! Clear your mind. Think of nothing. Pretend you are a mental-mute."

"Clear my mind…Mental-mute…Right. That shouldn't be hard," Gilbert murmured to himself and laughed. "What are those things hovering over there?"

"Those are sentinels. They are the eyes and ears for the Luminon's Xiocrom. This is where we are most at risk… so be on your guard," she warned.

"What is the Luminon?"

"The Luminon is our supreme leader. Luminon in our language means literally 'One Who Brings Light To All.'"

"Okay, and so, what is this Zio-crum thingy?"

"The 'ZIO-CROM' is the artificial intelligence that controls the government, bots, and the drone workforce. The Luminon uses it to maintain control over Mars."

"So your government is run by an artificial intelligence?"

"Yes. The Luminon had it constructed after he seized power. Before that, we had a democratically elected government — The Supreme Council of Twelve. The Supreme Council of Twelve was comprised of twelve Archons or administrators. The Luminon claimed that food shortages came as a result of corruption within our government. He believed that a centralized government run by an artificial intelligence could manage things better than our democratically elected officials could. He claimed that an artificial intelligence would never be swayed by greed or corruption like the council members who came before. We never used to have this degree of centralized control. The Xiocrom now controls the day-to-day operations of the government as well as manages the robot and drone workforces."

"Really? Are you directly controlled by the Xiocrom?"

"The watchers and the drones are the only elements of our society that are directly controlled by it — along with the sentinels and bots, of course. With practice, telepathy can be blocked. Again, try to avoid eye contact with people until we leave the checkpoint. You see over there—" Aoléon said as she pointed to the far corner of the atrium.

"What?" asked Gilbert.

"Over there, where you see a bit of air vibrating — looks like heat shimmering?" Gilbert peered closer. It took a second for his eyes to focus on the spot.

"Oh yeah, weird! What — is — that?" It looked like heat wavering off a road during a hot summer's day. When he squinted his eyes, he could partially see a translucent silhouette of a spherically shaped object appear.

"That is a cloaked sentinel. The sentinels are the eyes and ears of the Xiocrom."

"So, the sentinels can turn invisible?"

"Most of the time they remain cloaked, yes."

Standing adjacent to the checkpoint, several taller Martians stood guard wearing padded spacesuits with oversized boots, and they held extra-large weapons.

"Those guards of some kind?" Gilbert inquired as he motioned toward the checkpoint.

"Those are paladin guards, elite warriors who serve the Luminon."

It was finally time for them to enter the checkpoint. "Hold still for decontamination scan," announced a disembodied robotic voice.

Gilbert grimaced while clutching his privates, unsure what the effects of the scan might do to him. He heard Aoléon's voice in his head persuading him to relax.

A bright light passed over his body twice. A shiver shot down Gilbert's spine as the light passed over and through him. After a moment, the Martian security guards let them pass. Gilbert tried his best not to look embarrassed.

"You seemed a bit nervous," Aoléon added while taking Gilbert by the arm and leading him away from the checkpoint and into the spaceport.

"I guess that wasn't so bad. I was just worried that I might lose my…never mind." They both laughed.

Gilbert exhaled deeply with relief and moved quickly out of the decontamination checkpoint. Inside the spaceport, crowds of Martians moved to and fro along with half a dozen other alien species that came and went. Some were cephalopods with tentacles like a squid;

some were insectoid, resembling a giant praying mantis; and some were short with grey skin and huge black eyes. Gilbert didn't have time to examine them all because Aoléon whisked him through the spaceport at a brisk walking pace.

"More than thirty-one distinct alien species visit our city regularly, coming from all over the galaxy," explained Aoléon as she led Gilbert outside.

"Are you going to give me a tour?"

"We do not have time today because it is getting late, but I promise I will show you parts of the city on the way home — at least from the air."

Outside the spaceport, they boarded a Martian transport ship that resembled a bent metallic potato. It quickly filled up with twenty or so other passengers who varied in size and shape. All of them were preoccupied and didn't pay any attention to Gilbert. Despite this, Gilbert fidgeted and tried to avoid eye contact with the other passengers. The transport took off and entered the Martian megalopolis traffic stream. Gilbert sat next to Aoléon and gazed out of the portal window at the vast cityscape below. Aoléon sampled his thoughts and watched him as his eyes grew wide with amazement.

They flew by a giant craft that had an enormous holokron display broadcasting a picture of a Martian called "Konx-Om-Pax" and instructing all Martians to report his whereabouts if spotted. A couple of Martians began to discuss the possibility of Konx-Om-Pax's capture. Their mouths weren't moving, but Gilbert could nonetheless hear what they were thinking when he concentrated hard enough. They seemed to be talking about Konx-Om-Pax and the working conditions in the galact processing facilities. Whatever that meant.

"If they catch him, we are doomed," the taller Martian worker said to the other who sat across from him.

"Can you believe that?"

"And now rumors of a bot workforce — they will replace us all for sure," said his friend with a worried look.

Gilbert turned to Aoléon. "Is this Pax guy a criminal?"

Aoléon shook her head to indicate that they shouldn't be talking about this in public and whispered, "Not really.

He is sort of a spiritual leader who has spoken out against the rule of the Luminon."

The transport ship finally arrived at Aoléon's enclave at the outskirts of the giant megalopolis.

"Here we are," she stated. They exited the transport and headed toward her home, walking through the city streets.

"Normally we would phase to my house, but I wanted to show you the city."

"Phase?"

"Short for 'phased-matter-jump.' It allows us to transport instantly to anywhere we wish. But most of the time, when I am not in a hurry, I use my skyboard. It is much more fun. There is no better way to see the city than on a skyboard."

"What about walls? Can you actually phase through solid objects like walls?"

"Most of the time, yes. However, some walls are shielded — like in some high-security areas, and the shielding prohibits phasing."

"I see. Will you show me how to skyboard sometime?"

"Sure will. Maybe tomorrow after class."

"You mean I get to go to your school?"

"Yes! Tomorrow you will attend the Martian Space Academy with me."

"Zoikers! That's so cool!"

They walked down an artery between two towering buildings, and Gilbert observed Martians walking to and fro carrying babies and various items while being followed by hovering carts. Everyone moved with a purpose, yet no one spoke. Gilbert noticed that they seemed to behave almost like a hive of worker ants — part of a larger collective consciousness. Each had a job to do, and they were actively focused on completing the task at hand.

"Who are those Martians?" Gilbert pointed to a group that all seemed to look exactly the same to him except for their size.

"Those are drones — part of the worker caste."

"I hate to ask, but are they male or female? I sure can't tell."

"They are neither. They are androgynous — without reproductive capabilities."

"You're kidding!"

"No, no. They are cloned in a lab that way, and they are responsible for all the basic maintenance work that goes on in our society that is not done by robots."

"Sounds horrible! That's like slavery, isn't it?"

"It is primitive and cruel. The caste system and the drones were brought about by the Luminon's rise to power."

Aoléon and Gilbert turned a corner at one of the smaller buildings and headed down a narrow ventricle off the main artery. A lump of fur with three ping-pong-ball eyes attached to antennae ran up to Gilbert and started to sniff him. Gilbert screeched and jumped back from the creature. The animal's actions reminded him of the way dogs that craved attention behave. This creature was even weirder looking than the other aliens he had seen so far. He tried to back away, but the animal was too quick for him — it jumped up onto him and started to lick his face.

"I think it likes you."

"Ahh! Get it off me!" cried Gilbert. A suction cup tongue shot from the moog and stuck onto Gilbert's helmet as it tried to give him a kiss.

"Oh, it is just a pet — a moog — totally harmless!" Aoléon chortled.

"Uh huh…just keep it away from me, 'kay? I just hope nothing bursts from my chest!" Gilbert stared at the bug-eyed beast as it turned and scampered away, its goggling eyes bobbing up and down with each hop of its cucumber-shaped body. *Cute and luckily harmless,* thought Gilbert with relief.

As Aoléon and Gilbert walked a little farther, Gilbert noticed a Martian sitting against a curved wall of a building where just a moment ago there had been nothing at all. It was as if the Martian had just appeared out of thin air. Gilbert examined him closely. Something about him seemed different from the other Martians they had encountered. As they approached, the Martian stood up and raised a hand for them to stop.

"Greetings, Aoléon. I bring important news," the Martian spoke briskly.

"Deus ex machina!" Aoléon cried out. She jumped back, startled by the old Martian. "Y-You…you are Konx-Om-Pax! But, h-how do you know me?"

Gilbert recognized him as the Martian he had seen being broadcast over the holokron as a wanted criminal. Gilbert watched them quietly, not quite sure what to make of this peculiar exchange. The Martian didn't strike Gilbert as being overtly dangerous, even though he was on the Martian equivalent to the FBI's most wanted list. But then again, this was the second Martian that he had ever met face to face, and sometimes appearances could be deceiving.

"You may address me simply as Pax. You may not yet realize it, but you possess great strength, as does he — the Terran boy," Pax said, motioning toward Gilbert.

Gilbert choked on his own saliva and stumbled back-ward. *How does he know who I am?* he thought to himself, unnerved by this strange Martian. *I just got here, and already they know.*

"Relax, my Terran friend," Pax said eyeing Gilbert who stood ill at ease. "Your secret is safe." He looked steadily at Aoléon. "You and the Terran boy must work together to gather intelligence about the Luminon's plans. After we have gathered enough evidence, we can then expose the Luminon, stop the invasion of Terra and regain control of Mars. *You have been chosen.*"

"Chosen?" sputtered Aoléon looking shocked.

"You and that prince dude from Nigeria both take a number and get in line."

"Prince dude from Nigeria? Who is that?" whispered Aoléon with a sideward glance.

"You know, there is a prince from the country Nigeria, which I think is in Asia somewhere…Well, you probably don't know because you are a Martian. But he once sent me an e-mail stating that I was special and had been chosen and that he would transfer a million dollars into my bank account if only I could help him out…," Gilbert chortled. "Anyway, I never got the money."

As they spoke, a sentinel silently flew overhead unnoticed and observed their conversation.

Turning back toward Pax, Aoléon replied, "This is silly. You must have me confused with someone else. I am just an ordinary Martian girl," she protested.

"Be like a star and illuminate the world. You have the ability within yourself, Aoléon, to shine a light into the darkness and expose this great evil. Your family and all of Mars are depending on you. Just as the Terrans are depending on this boy, though they may never realize it."

"But why?" asked Aoléon, unsettled. Gilbert's expression mirrored her own confusion.

"We know that the Luminon is developing an invasion force — we believe to conquer Terra and to capture its milk cows. It is up to you to gather proof of his plans so that the people of Mars may know what his true intentions are before it is too late. If you should fail, many innocents will die, the Luminon and his legions of darkness will prevail, and all that we know and love will be lost forever. Go quickly now and may the Creator watch over you."

"Is this some strange dream?" Aoléon murmured under her breath.

As Aoléon reached out to touch Pax, he illuminated and transformed into a bright glowing ball of energy. Aoléon and Gilbert collapsed as Pax vanished in a flash of light.

"What…what just happened?" Gilbert cried out.

"Pax…that was Konx-Om-Pax — considered a great prophet and spiritual leader on Mars — or possibly a couple of meteors short of an asteroid field."

"Do you trust him?"

"Do you? Come. It is late," said Aoléon as she headed down the alley at a faster pace. Gilbert had to jog just to keep up with her, but he found jogging effortless in his new Martian spacesuit. It seemed to be following the commands of his legs and giving him extra speed. As he ran after Aoléon, the invisible sentinel continued to track them from overhead.

## Continue the saga in
## Part Two: "The Luminess of Mars"

# GLOSSARY

**A.I.** — An abbreviation for *artificial intelligence* — a thinking, sentient machine or computer.

**A. I. hacking** — Breaking into and manipulating artificial intelligence (see **A.I.**) to do your bidding.

**AU** — An abbreviation for *Astronomical Unit*. An Astronomical Unit is the mean distance between the Earth and the Sun. In 2012, the International Astronomical Union defined the distance to be 149,597,870,700 meters or about 93 million miles.

**arcologies** — Enormous, raised-pyramid hyperstructures that are self-contained microcities in a single, gargantuan building. They combine high population density residential habitats with self-contained commercial, food, agricultural, waste, energy, and transportation facilities.

**Aurora Interceptor** — A fictional interceptor version that I created for this book of the U.S. Air Force Aurora spy plane. "Aurora" was the code name for the U.S. Air Force's replacement for the SR-71 spy plane. The Aurora went into service in 1989. It was capable of flying into space without aid of rocket boosters, orbiting the Earth, and landing on the ground. It could fly at speeds in excess of Mach 12 within the atmosphere.

**bovars** — Martian cows that are saurian in origin, hatched from eggs, and produce a milk-like substance used in making galact (see **galact**), the main foodstuff of the Martian people.

**Ciakar** — A term used for *Draco Prime* — the Draconian (see **Draconian**) ruling caste. A Ciakar can range from 14 feet to 22 feet tall (4.3 meters to 7 meters tall) and can weigh up to 1,800 pounds (816 kg). The most distinguishing features of the Ciakar, the supreme leader of the Draconians, are white scales and large dragon wings — features that the other subcastes of the Draconian race do not possess. This is what distinguishes the Ciakar as royalty among the dragon race. A Ciakar also possesses some psionic power — telepathy and telekinesis; however, it is not nearly as strong as in some of the other alien races.

**CQB** — An abbreviation for *close quarters battle*. CQB is the art of tactical combat while indoors.

**Deimos** — See **Phobos and Deimos**.

**Draconian** — A reptiloid species originating from the constellation Orion. They were the first sentient species in our galaxy to have interstellar space travel (more than four billion years ago). Their society is based on a hierarchical caste system in which the leaders constitute a separate species known as the Ciakar (see **Ciakar**). The castes are royalty, priest, soldier, worker, and outcast.

**Draco Prime** — See **Ciakar.**

**DUMB** — An abbreviation for *Deep Underground Military Base*.

**EBE** — An abbreviation for *Extraterrestrial Biological Entity* — another term for alien.

**ESA** — An abbreviation for *European Space Agency* (NASA for Europe).

**FBI** — An abbreviation for *Federal Bureau of Investigation.*

**galact** — A milk-like substance that is the primary food for the Martian people.

**GSG-9** — An abbreviation for *Grenzschutzgruppe 9*. GSG-9 is the elite counter-terrorism and special operations unit of the German Federal Police.

**holokron display / holokronic display** — A holographic projector and communications device.

**Luminess** — The spouse of the Luminon.

**Luminon** — The supreme ruler of Mars.

**Majestic Twelve (MJ-12)** — A secret committee of scientists, military leaders, and government officials formed in 1947 by an executive order of U.S. President Harry S. Truman to investigate UFO activity in the aftermath of the Roswell crash incident.

**MAJIC** — See **Majestic Twelve**.

**MJ-12** — See **Majestic Twelve**.

**nanites** — Microscopic robots that perform various enhancement actions.

**NASA** — An abbreviation for *National Aeronautics and Space Administration*.

**NOFORN** — An abbreviation for *no foreign nationals*. NOFORN is a designation for classified documents that means that no foreign nationals should be permitted to see them.

**NSA** — An abbreviation for *National Security Agency*. The three-letter alphabet soup agency is lovingly called "no such agency" by its spook insiders. It is responsible for running the global ECHELON System — a signal intelligence-gathering network that sucks up and records all phone, satellite, Internet, and data worldwide.

**NYPD** — An abbreviation for *New York Police Department*.

**omnitool** — A hand-held computer device that can perform a multitude of functions including being able to hack door locks as well as deactivate force fields and turrets.

**omniverse** — The conceptual ensemble of all possible universes with all possible laws of physics.

**ORCON** — An abbreviation for *originator controlled*. ORCON is the intelligence marking signaling that material contained is "originator-controlled" and cannot be distributed further without the National Security Agency's permission.

**paladins** — See **Royal Paladin Elite Guards**.

**parsec** — A unit of astronomical distance in which 1 parsec = 3.26 light years or about 19 trillion miles, 1 mega-parsec =1 million parsecs or 3.262 million light years, and 1 light year = the distance light travels in one year. Long story short, it is a ludicrous distance to travel so quickly because it is a distance far beyond most people's ability to comprehend.

**phase-jump** — See **phase-matter jump**.

**phase-matter jump** — The ability to shift to the post-plasma beam state of matter and teleport yourself and others instantly to another location using only your mind.

**phase-shifting** — See **phasing**.

**phasing** — The ability to shift or change matter states. See also **phase-matter jump**.

**Phobos and Deimos (moons)** — The two moons of Mars that are named after the two horses of the Greek god of war meaning "fear" and "dread." They are roughly the size of large asteroids and have artificially circular orbits around the equator of Mars. The ratio of Phobos's orbital period to Deimos's orbital period is almost clock-like in that Phobos is the minute hand and Deimos the hour hand. Deimos orbits once every 30.4 hours and Phobos every 7 hours 39 minutes.

**plasma** — The fourth state of matter. A state of matter in which atoms and molecules are so hot that they ionize and break up into their constituent parts: negatively charged electrons and positively charged ions.

**Royal Paladin Elite Guards** — The select guards of the Luminon.

**Schwarzschild radius** — The variable radius setting that determines the size of the micro-singularity. The higher the setting, the larger the event horizon and, subsequently, the greater the area of destruction. Dialed down to its lowest setting, it could target a single individual within a crowd while leaving the others unharmed. At its maximum setting, it could destroy an entire planet. Note to operator: using this weapon at its maximum setting is inadvisable.

**sentinels** — Flying robotic sentries that guard Martian airspace around the megalopolis and conduct reconnaissance for the Xiocrom. Most of the time, the sentinels remain cloaked or invisible.

**sentrybot** — A security robot designed for basic policing and guard duty. It is less powerful than a soldierbot.

**singularity** — A singularity is associated with black holes. It is a situation in which matter is forced to be compressed to a point (a space-like singularity).

**SITREP** — An abbreviation for *situation report.*

**Terra / Terrans** — Terms that mean *Earth / Earthlings* and refer to the Earth and / or to people who inhabit the Earth.

**umbra (classification)** — The highest level of classification.

**VTOL** — An abbreviation for *Vertical Takeoff and Landing.* VTOL refers to an aircraft that is capable of lifting off like a helicopter and then transitioning to regular flight like an airplane.

**Xiocrom** — The artificial intelligence that controls all Martian governmental functions, the bot and drone workforces, and the robot invasion forces.

*Note: Many of the above definitions came from Wikipedia, the free online encyclopedia. I would like to thank their many anonymous authors whose explanations have contributed to the project.*

*For Xena, who kept me company and
made me laugh while I spent countless hours working on
this book. For Dad, who helped me when times were tough,
and for Mom and Aunt Gwen, who helped edit numerous
drafts of this book. And for Jennifer, who inspired me
to make the lead character female.*

CPSIA information can be obtained at www.ICGtesting.com
Printed in the USA
LVOW05*0850140815

450124LV00010B/25/P